Ziggy
and
The Black Dinosaurs™

SHADOWS
of
CAESAR'S
CREEK

by Sharon M. Draper

Just Us Books, Inc.
East Orange, New Jersey

Special thanks to:
Carol Fassig—Caesar Creek State Park
Chief Hawk Pope
Sun Spirit Lowe
All the members of the Shawnee tribe who treated me with such
kindness and respect at Shawandassee in 1995 and 1996.
Nanine L. Martinez
Nancye Caesar Donaldson
The entire Caesar family—all the many descendants of Caesar who
treated me so warmly at the Caesar Family Reunion in 1996.

Do shadows really walk at midnight?

The noise in the bushes behind them got louder and closer. The animal had tracked them and was only a few feet behind them. It was just a matter of time.

Ziggy broke a speed record. He ignored branches and scratches and even his fear of the darkness. He didn't know where he was heading anymore. He was lost, and afraid, and out of breath. In the moonlight, he could see the shadows of the trees ahead. He ran for the tree straight in front of him, hoping to try to climb it, hoping this bear didn't know it was supposed to be able to climb up after him.

Suddenly, the tree moved! Standing straight and tall in front of him now were the shadows of two trees—and one of them was moving toward him.

Ziggy screamed and tried to turn, but the branches of the tall shadow tree reached out and grabbed his wrist....

CHAPTER 1

Ziggy's thoughts bounced like hot popcorn as he ran through his backyard to the clubhouse of The Black Dinosaurs. *An overnight camping trip*! he thought with excitement. *Fishing! Hiking! Cooking over a campfire!* He couldn't wait to tell Rico, Rashawn and Jerome, the other members of The Black Dinosaurs, about the letter from Camp Caesar.

Ziggy's huge backyard was wonderful. It was a place where flowers, weeds, rabbits, and ten-year-old boys could grow wild. It was a place to dream and create—a perfect location for secrets and adventures. Ziggy followed a path, probably used by raccoons, which ran back into the thick underbrush to their clubhouse.

Using the remains of an old fence that the boys had found in Ziggy's back yard, they had built the clubhouse themselves last summer. The Black Dinosaurs had cut holes that looked a lot like windows in the two side walls, and for the front door, they used a smaller section of the fence wall. It closed with a bent piece of wire coat hanger.

Inside, the clubhouse was about ten feet by twelve feet—not really big—but large enough for four boys to sit and talk. In it was one lawn chair with most of the webbing missing, one folding chair left over from a church picnic, one three-legged kitchen chair (they used a large rock to balance it), and a bicycle with two flat tires. This was their seating arrangement, or, they could push those aside and sit on the blanket that Ziggy's mom had given them.

Just as Ziggy got to the clubhouse, he tripped over his shoelace, lost his balance, landed on his backside, and rolled with a laugh to the three-legged kitchen chair that held Jerome. Ziggy never walked anywhere—he bounced, or jogged or galloped wherever he went. He was always in a good mood, always excited about whatever was happening around him. So Jerome was not surprised when Ziggy landed at his feet, bubbling with news.

He helped Ziggy up, and asked with a laugh,

"What's up, Ziggy?"

"Just wait till you hear, mon! Where are Rico and Rashawn?" Behind him, they could hear the rustling of something in the bushes.

Rashawn's Siberian Husky, whose name was Afrika, and who had one blue eye and one brown eye, trotted out of the bushes, found his favorite spot under a tree, and went to sleep. Rashawn, tall, brown, skinny, and wearing his favorite army boots, stomped through the backyard and sat down on a large rock in front of the clubhouse.

"What's goin' on, fellas?" he asked. "Where's Rico?"

Ziggy was still hopping with excitement. He wore a green vest, blue shirt, and bright red jeans. A large knitted cap covered his braids today, which usually bounced as much as he did. Ziggy's family had come from Jamaica to Ohio several years ago, and had moved on the street where Rico, Rashawn, and Jerome lived. The four boys had been friends since first grade.

Rico crawled out of the window of the clubhouse. He had a huge wad of bubble gum in his mouth and was attempting to blow the world's biggest bubble. He walked slowly, concentrating on blowing and balancing the bubble, which was almost the size of his face. He didn't see Ziggy, who leaped in the air, bursting to tell his good news.

"Guess what!" cried Ziggy. As Ziggy began to speak, he lifted his arms in excitement. At that moment, Rico and his bubble walked right into Ziggy's hand. "Splat!" went the bubble gum, and Rico's surprised face and thick brown hair were instantly covered with sticky, pink bubble gum.

Rashawn and Jerome hooted with laughter; Ziggy rolled on the ground with delight. Rico didn't laugh much. But he smiled as he sat on the grass, picking gum out of his hair.

"That bubble would have gone in the book of records," he said with fake disappointment. "I bet it was the biggest one in the world so far!"

"Aw mon, I blow bubbles bigger than that every day!" boasted Ziggy. "But you gotta mix the bubble gum with mashed potatoes first! That's the secret ingredient!"

"Yuck!" laughed the others. They were used to Ziggy's unusual tastes in food. He stirred his chocolate milk with pickles and he put mustard on his corn flakes.

"So tell us, Ziggy," Jerome said finally. "What's the big news?"

"The mailman just left," Ziggy whispered with excitement, "and the letter from Camp Caesar came today! It's all set! We're going on a camping trip to Caesar's Creek State Park next week!"

Rashawn cheered. "Let's hear it for my dad! I knew his club would pull it together!" Rashawn's dad was a member of the Black Heritage Club. They had decided several months ago to provide field trips for the young people of the community and this camping trip was one of the first activities.

"I've never slept outside in the woods before," admitted Jerome. I wonder what we ought to take."

Ziggy pulled a folded piece of paper from the back pocket of his red jeans. "Not to worry, mon!" he announced, "Here's the list of things to bring—let's see here .... flashlights, sleeping bags, back packs, extra socks, bug spray . . . ."

"Bug spray?" said Jerome in pretended alarm. Jerome hated insects. Every day he carried bug spray in his school book bag, just in case. "You know how I am about bugs! I'll probably never get to sleep, looking for bugs in the night."

Ziggy laughed and said once again, "Not to worry, mon! It will be so dark in those woods at night that you'll never even see the bugs that bite you!"

Jerome picked up a handful of dry leaves and threw them at Ziggy. "Hey, you really know how to make a dude feel better, man!"

"Who's going?" asked Rico, who had almost finished pulling the bubble gum out of his hair.

"The four of us, of course, mon, and four other kids from school. I think there might be other kids near the campsite from other schools, my mum said," replied Ziggy.

"Any girls?" asked Rashawn.

"Who cares, mon!" Ziggy laughed. "I'm more concerned with the lions and tigers and bears!"

"There are no lions and tigers in Ohio," Rico declared. "But I'm not sure about bears."

"Bears?" asked Rashawn fearfully.

"There's no bears around here," Jerome stated, "but I know the woods are full of bugs!"

"Don't forget we'll have the bug spray," reminded Rico.

"Bug spray won't do much against a bear!" muttered Rashawn, who didn't want to admit he was a little worried.

Ziggy checked the list again. "Not to worry, mon," he announced with cheerful assurance, "nothing on here about bears!"

"That doesn't mean there aren't any," Rashawn continued, smiling in spite of himself.

"What about Indians?" asked Rico.

"I don't know," Jerome said with a frown. "There used to be millions of Indians in Ohio—a long time ago."

"I wonder what happened to all of them," wondered Rico.

"Hey, mon, I bet there are thousands of Indians living in the woods up there right now!"

"No, Ziggy," Rico said thoughtfully, "I think they got pushed out—from their own land." My dad told me that it used to be really beautiful around here before there were roads or bridges or even houses."

"Can you imagine," Rashawn thought out loud, "nothing but forests for miles and miles? The Indians had it so good!"

"Yeah, except for one thing," grinned Jerome.

"What, mon?"

"There was no place to stop for hamburgers and french fries!"

"Or pizza!"

"Or tacos!"

"Or chocolate-covered spaghetti, mon!"

At that, they all grabbed dry leaves and grass from the yard and threw it at Ziggy, until he ran laughing and shouting, through the backyard.

"Not to worry, mon!" they heard him yell in the distance, still laughing, "I'll bring my own!"

CHAPTER 2

The following Saturday dawned bright and clear. Jerome, wearing his uncle's tall black hiking boots and black leather vest, waited in the parking lot with his grandmother and his two little sisters, Temika and LaTonya. They were still sleepy, and a little grumpy that they had been made to get up just so Jerome could go on a trip. But nobody argued with Granny. When she said "get up," that's what you did.

Jerome's backpack and sleeping bag, which were a faded Army green, had belonged to his grandfather, who had fought in the Vietnam War. Jerome wore dark sunglasses and tried not to look excited as the camp bus pulled into the lot.

Rico's mom drove a dull brown car that badly needed a muffler and a paint job. It rattled and sputtered and coughed into the parking lot, just behind the bus. Rico grinned at Jerome and hopped out of the car almost before it stopped. He was dressed in blue jeans and a matching blue shirt, which was, as usual, neatly tucked in. He even had a matching blue sleeping bag and backpack.

Jerome knew without looking that Rico's backpack would have neat rolls of clothes, with a toothbrush in a plastic holder and extra plastic bags for wet socks. The others sometimes teased Rico because of his organization, but they knew that they could depend on him to build anything they needed—from clubhouses to tree bridges.

The other children going on the trip quickly began to fill the parking lot. Tiana was a tall, pretty girl who always had a smile for Rashawn. She had once helped to save the Black Dinosaurs when they were trapped in an underground tunnel. Portia, a petite, cinnamon brown girl with long black braids, ate math problems for breakfast, everyone said. She never got anything less than an A in any math class and had already skipped to the seventh grade book.

Liza was the fastest runner in the school, and everyone knew that she could also beat up any kid in the school—boy or girl. She smiled easily and would give her last gummy bear to a friend, but she had a quick temper and broke her pencils when she got mad. Her best friend Brandy wrote poetry. She always carried a pencil and paper with her to jot down ideas. Brandy had a fondness for jelly beans and always kept some in her book bag.

"Is everyone here?" asked the bus driver.

Rico looked at Jerome and started to say, "Ziggy—" But piercing the silence of the morning, a police siren screamed in the distance. Everyone in the parking lot turned to look as the sound of the siren got closer. Suddenly speeding around the corner, a police car roared into the parking lot, with lights flashing, sirens roaring, and Rashawn and Ziggy waving from the two back windows.

Everyone cheered and crowded around the police car, which was driven by Rashawn's dad. Rashawn was proud that his dad was a cop, and even prouder that he had broken the rules to drive them to the parking lot in such a blaze of glory.

"Thanks, Dad," Rashawn whispered as he climbed out of the police car. His dad smiled.

Ziggy got out of the police car slowly, grinning and waving to the cheering crowd of his friends. "Not to worry, mon! Ziggy is here!" he said dramatically. He was dressed in his favorite jeans, and a huge purple coat that came almost to the tops of his new green tennis shoes. The coat had belonged to Ziggy's cousin and was filled with large pockets, small pockets, zippers, and flaps.

"Where's your backpack, Ziggy?" asked Rico.

"It's right here, mon," replied Ziggy with a grin, pointing to his coat. "I've got socks in this pocket, a clean t-shirt here, and a peanut butter and pickle sandwich in this one! Everything a mon needs for a camping trip is right here in my coat pockets!"

Noni, the counselor from Camp Caesar, dressed in the light brown uniform of the Ohio State Department of Parks and Recreation, looked tanned and tough. She wore her hair in one long black braid tied with a piece of leather.

"She looks like an Indian maiden," Tiana whispered to Portia.

Noni checked her list and announced loudly, "Campers, load the bus now. Stow your gear in the overhead racks. Let's head out of here!"

Rico's mom gave him a quick hug and a final warning, "Be careful, now! Have fun!" Rico wondered how he could do both, but he just nodded and ran to the bus. The girls boarded the bus next, looking at the boys, but refusing to sit anywhere near them.

Rashawn got his gear from the back of the police car, gave a final wave to his dad, and headed for the bus. "See you tomorrow, Dad! Don't tell Mom I left my winter coat in your car!"

His dad grinned. "I don't think you'll need it. Go on and don't worry about it. She worries enough for the three of us!" Rashawn gave his father a look of thanks and stomped his heavy army boots cheerfully onto the bus.

Ziggy was the last to board the bus. His purple coat flapped behind him in the early morning breeze as he jogged around the parking lot one last time.

"Let's go, Ziggy," called Noni. "Where is your sleeping bag?"

Ziggy stopped suddenly. "Oh no!" he exclaimed. "I left it at home, mon! I was so excited about riding in the police car that I forgot it. Let's see, I hugged my mum, put my hat on, fed my cat on the front porch—it's on my porch!"

Noni sighed, looked at her watch, and said, "Well, Ziggy. . . ."

Just then, Ziggy's mom pulled into the parking lot. His face brightened as he ran to the car. She shook her head as if to say, "When will you learn, Ziggy?", but she smiled as if she knew that it wouldn't be the last time he would forget.

"Oh thanks, Mum! You're the best! I promise I'll never do this again! Not to worry!" He hugged her through the car window, kissed her on the cheek, and leaped onto the bus. He waved and grinned at her from the window, and even blew her a kiss. She had no choice but to laugh.

Finally, Noni told the driver to close the doors and take off. Everyone cheered as the bus roared out of the parking lot, leaving the parents waving behind them.

As the bus lumbered down the highway, the signs and sights of the city began to disappear.

Trees and fields and cows soon replaced houses and stores and people.

"Look, mon!" cried Ziggy as he looked out of the window of the bus. "A deer! With antlers! Oh, wow! There's three—no, four—wait! I see six of them!" Everyone crowded to Ziggy's side of the bus to see. The small herd of deer looked up briefly, then darted into the thick woods behind them.

It's gonna be a good trip, thought Ziggy with satisfaction as he settled back into his seat.

The ride from their school to Caesar's Creek State Park only took about forty-five minutes. Before they knew it, the bus was turning down a small road. Straight ahead the children could see a large brown sign that read: CAESAR'S CREEK STATE PARK—5 MILES.

Ziggy bounced on his seat with excitement. Rico looked at Jerome and grinned. Rashawn looked at Tiana, but she was busy looking out of the window, or at least she pretended to be.

"Hey Noni!" Ziggy yelled from the back of the bus. "How come we got a park in Ohio named for Julius Caesar? Did he sleep here or something?"

"I'm glad you asked that, Ziggy," Noni replied with a smile. "Everyone listen up!" The bus got quiet for a moment and Noni stood in the middle of the aisle, swaying with the bus as it turned down the narrow roads that led to the camp. She asked loudly, "Does anyone know where Caesar's Creek got its name?

"Julius Caesar fell in a creek here?" Rashawn asked. Tiana giggled.

"Nope," Noni grinned.

"Julius Caesar discovered it?" asked Portia.

"Not even close!" Noni chuckled. "As a matter of fact, it wasn't named for Julius Caesar at all! Any more guesses?"

"Maybe it was named for Caesar's wife!" exclaimed Liza. The girls all laughed and agreed.

"Sorry, girls," Noni replied. "That's not it either."

"So who was it named for, Noni?" asked Jerome.

"Listen. . . ." she whispered with a mysterious voice. The bus had slowed to a stop. "Caesar's

Creek really was named for a man named Caesar. And this Caesar was a mighty, mighty man." She paused for a moment.

Ziggy had moved several seats closer so he could hear Noni better. He loved mysteries and stories about heroes.

Noni continued, the excitement building in her voice as she watched the faces of the children on the bus.

"Caesar was a Black man—an African American, an ex-slave, an explorer, and an Indian chief! And this was his valley, land given to him by the Shawnee Indians!"

She waved her arms and pointed toward the thick greenery all around them. At that, the door of the bus opened.

"Awesome, mon!" whispered Ziggy as he jumped from the top step of the bus to the grass-covered gravel. "Awesome!"

CHAPTER 3

The bus was finally unloaded and everyone stood blinking in the bright sunlight, quiet for a moment, looking up at the tall trees and into the shadows of the deep green forest in the distance. Birds chirped, the trees swayed in the soft breeze, and squirrels chased each other on the thin branches. Fifty feet from where they stood, a small pond rippled slightly in the morning sunshine.

"Looks like a postcard!" whispered Portia. "It's so quiet and pretty!"

"And all of this belonged to this dude named Caesar?" asked Rashawn in amazement. "How did he get here? Where did he come from?" And why did the Shawnees give it to him?"

"I'll answer all of your questions tonight at the campfire," Noni promised. "But first we have to get settled at our campsite."

"Where's our cabins, Noni?" asked Brandy. "It's pretty out here, but all I see is forest!"

"Sorry, Brandy," Noni answered, "no cabins for this trip. We're going to pitch our tents and sleep in the open air!"

"Cool!" she replied. "Maybe I'll write a poem about the 'murky midnight air'!"

"Open air!" gasped Jerome. "You mean where bugs can crawl on you at night?"

"Bugs gotta sleep, too, mon!" Ziggy offered. "Not to worry!"

Noni decided it was time to show them a little of nature up close. "Come over here," she said as she walked to the pond. They followed as she walked close to the edge of the pond, near the tall, reedy plants that grew in the water. "I want you to tell me what you see."

"I see water," said Tiana. "And look! I can see your reflection, Rico. You, too, Rashawn," she added shyly.

"I see bushes growing in the water," added Brandy.

"And leaves floating on the water—almost like they were growing there!" observed Portia.

"You're right," smiled Noni. "Those are

water lilies. Keep looking."

"I see bugs flying real close to the water—they look like little dive bombers!" admitted Jerome as he watched them. "They don't look so bad."

"There's a little fish in the water, too!" cried Rico. "Look! There's a whole bunch of them!"

"I don't see anything, mon!" moaned Ziggy. All of a sudden he jumped with excitement and cried, "I see a frog!" It's green and fat and I bet I can catch it!" Just as he lunged for the frog, Noni caught him by the tail of his purple coat.

"Not so fast, Ziggy!" she warned. "What are you going to do if you catch it?"

"Uh, I'll put it in a jar—or a cage—or, I don't know, just keep it, mon!"

"And then what?" Noni asked gently.

"I'll feed it!" Ziggy replied.

"What do frogs eat?" Noni continued.

"Worms, I guess, mon—and bugs! Hundreds of them!" Ziggy said firmly.

"And you're going to catch hundreds of bugs and worms for your frog every day?" The other kids were beginning to smile.

"Hundreds?"

"Frogs get very hungry," Noni grinned.

"Well, maybe I'll just let this little frog catch his own dinner tonight, mon," admitted Ziggy. "But I could have caught him if I wanted to!" Everyone laughed as the frog jumped just at that moment with a huge splash into the water.

"Okay, everyone," laughed Noni, "grab your gear and let's head for the campsite. We've got a long walk, then we have to set up our tents." Everyone groaned, but they gathered their packs and bags and followed Noni down a path into the woods.

"How far is it?" asked Rashawn after only a few minutes. "It seems so different from when we're at home and walking around the neighborhood."

"Just a couple of miles," replied Noni cheerfully. "Don't worry about the distance—just look around you as we walk and check out my neighborhood!"

The woods were much cooler and darker than the bright sunny pond they had just left.

Above them, the sky was sometimes completely covered by dark, green leaves. Crunchy pine needles and old, fallen leaves covered the path they followed.

Jerome took off his sunglasses and tucked them into his backpack. He and Rico wore hiking boots, and Rashawn was comfortable in his army boots. But Ziggy wore his bright green tennis shoes. The soles were soft, and along with the sounds of the birds and the crickets, Ziggy's "OUCH, MON!" echoed through the forest.

Liza was the only one who really seemed to enjoy the hike. She kept up with Noni and breathed deeply the fresh outdoor air. Brandy seemed to enjoy it, too, but she was looking at the woods and birds for ideas, not for her health. She gobbled jelly beans as they walked, dropping a few every now and then. Tiana stayed either just in front of, or just behind Rashawn, but he pretended to ignore her.

Noni walked slowly, pointing out the names of trees as they followed—oak, maple, birch, elm, and more. She showed them owl and deer droppings, and told them how they could tell the difference and what they could learn about an animal from that.

"Yuck!" squealed Tiana. "That's disgusting!"

"Everything's gotta poop, mon!" Ziggy explained cheerfully. "What's the big deal?"

"You're gross, Ziggy!" Brandy accused. He just laughed, ran off the path, and bumped into a tree. His long purple coat had gotten too warm, so he tied it around his waist by the sleeves. He spotted a leafy green plant next to him, so he broke off a piece and offered it to Brandy.

"Here!" he teased. He bowed like he had seen men do in movies, and offered her the plant as if it were a beautiful bouquet. "Write something beautiful about my green gift!"

Noni turned around then and yelled, "Ziggy! Throw that down! It's poison ivy!"

Ziggy tossed the plant into the trees and screamed. "I touched it! I'm gonna die, mon!" He fell on the ground, rolled on his back, and kicked his arms and legs.

Noni laughed and shook her head. "Is he

always like this?" she asked the rest of the kids.

"Usually, he's worse!" laughed Liza and Rico.

Noni got Ziggy up, brushed the leaves off his clothes, and washed his hands off with an alcohol wipe. "You might get a rash, Ziggy, but there's a chance you won't have any reaction at all."

"How do we know if it's poison ivy?" asked Jerome. "All this stuff looks the same to me.

"Poison ivy has leaves with three points on them. Try this—'Leaves of three—watch out for me'."

Ziggy was much quieter now. He stayed on the path right behind Noni. He kept looking at his hands.

"Whatcha doin'?" asked Rico.

"I'm checking to see if my hands are gonna fall off, mon!"

Noni gave Ziggy a hug. "You'll be fine. 'Not to worry!' Isn't that what you always say?"

Ziggy grinned and relaxed a little. But he still checked his hands when Noni wasn't looking.

"What's that plant, Noni?" Portia asked,

pointing to a large, leafy plant growing close to the ground. "There sure is a lot of it."

"That's called May apple, Portia. See this fruit growing underneath the leaves? It can be eaten, but the leaves are poisonous!"

"Poisonous?" Tiana repeated.

"If you touch the leaves, like poison ivy?" asked Rico.

"No, you have to chew the leaves. I'm told they are very bitter. You'd never eat them by accident."

"Who would want to do that?" Brandy asked. She had started on her second bag of jelly beans.

"The stories say that the Indians around here would chew the leaves of the May apple if they got captured by the settlers!" Noni explained.

"I would hate to be captured!" Rashawn exclaimed. "To be tied up or locked up would be awful!"

"Kinda like Ziggy's frog, huh?" Tiana replied.

"Right."

"Can you imagine what it was like a long time ago when the Indians lived here?" Tiana spoke softly, looking around at the quiet beauty around her. "It's so pretty!"

"And a little scary, too!" Portia added.

"I can almost feel the shadows of the Indians who walked here a long time ago," Brandy said dramatically.

"I would love to have been an Indian boy!" Rico said strongly. "Just hunting and fishing and playing in the woods all day!"

"I wonder if Indian boys ever got poison ivy, mon," Ziggy said quietly, starting to scratch his left arm.

CHAPTER 4

They walked through the woods slowly, looking at birds and flowers that Noni pointed out,
laughing and shouting at each other.

"You'd never make it as young Indians,"
laughed Noni. "You're much too noisy! A young
Shawnee boy could walk through the deepest part
of these woods and never even snap a twig!"

"Well, Shawnee boys didn't wear hiking
boots like Jerome," Portia answered.

"Or bright green tennis shoes like Ziggy!"
added Brandy.

"I'm gonna pretend I'm an Indian brave," declared Jerome.

"Well you better go catch that squirrel for dinner, mon!" laughed Ziggy.

"I'm getting hungry, Noni," complained
Ziggy. "When can we eat? Are we almost there?"

"Look!" Noni replied with pride.

The path had widened, and the trees disappeared behind them. The children stopped sud-

denly, amazed and silenced by what they saw. They stood on the edge of a huge meadow. The bright sun, after the dim shadows of the woods, made the meadow shine with a golden glow. A path had been broken through the tall grasses. At the end of the path on the other side of the meadow lay a large blue lake.

"Wow!" exclaimed Rashawn. "Cool!"

"It's another postcard moment," Tiana remarked with a smile.

Brandy stopped eating her jelly beans long enough to pull out her notebook. She scribbled a few words, then stood silently, breathing the sweet crisp air.

Ziggy didn't have time for poetic moments. He rushed past the rest of them, and ran down the path toward the lake. "Whoopie!" he cried. "Let's go fishing!"

"You probably scared away every fish for a hundred miles," called Noni. "Let's get these tents up first. We'll set them up in this clearing—girls' tent over here—boys' tent over there. We'll make our campfire in the middle."

Noni had been carrying the two tents on her pack. She showed them how easy it was to change the small folded objects into tents. Rashawn and Jerome helped her with the stakes, while Portia and Tiana pulled and wrapped the rope. Rico and Ziggy went to collect twigs for the fire, while Brandy and Liza unrolled the sleeping bags and unpacked the food.

"Where are you gonna sleep, Noni?" Liza asked.

"Since this is the larger tent, I'll sleep with the girls," she replied.

"Well, who's gonna protect us?" Jerome inquired. "Suppose a bear comes and kidnaps us while you're sleeping?"

"You've got Ziggy," Noni replied with a laugh. "No bear would dare to bother you!"

Ziggy and Rico returned just then. Each carried an armload of sticks. "What's so funny, mon?" Ziggy asked with a grin.

"Oh, nothing," giggled Portia. "Just thinking about what Ziggybear soup might taste like!"

"Yummy, of course, mon!" Ziggy grinned

as he dumped the pile of sticks right near Portia's foot.

"Sorry, no Ziggybear soup today," laughed Noni, "but let's eat lunch. You all have worked very hard this morning."

"All right!" cheered Rashawn with glee. He pulled a large, overstuffed brown paper lunch bag out of his backpack. He dumped the contents on the grass in front of him—a bag of potato chips, three cheese sandwiches, an apple, an orange, a large plastic bottle of juice, and six chocolate cookies.

"How many did you pack for, Rashawn?" asked Rico. "You got enough there for an army."

"It will take an army to get it from me," mumbled Rashawn as he bit into the apple. "I'm hungry!"

"Do you want to trade one of those cheese sandwiches for my ham sandwich?" Tiana asked Rashawn.

Rashawn shook his head. His mouth was too full to reply. Jerome told her, "Naw, you keep it. He won't trade. Rashawn doesn't eat meat."

"Oh, yeah, I forgot," Tiana muttered. She felt a little embarrassed.

Rashawn grinned at her. "Don't worry about it. I'll take one of your cupcakes for a chocolate cookie, though," he said offering it to her.

Rico and Ziggy giggled. They knew that Rashawn didn't give up his chocolate cookies for anybody. Tiana just smiled as she nibbled at the cookie.

Ziggy's lunch was a sight to behold. Each of the pockets of the purple coat held something different. First he pulled out his peanut butter and pickle sandwich and sat it in front of him. From another pocket he pulled a grapefruit. From a pocket with a zipper came a bottle of juice—prune juice. In a large, buttoned pocket, wrapped in foil, he had hidden four large pancakes. Two were covered with jelly; two were covered with ketchup. Finally, he pulled what looked like the largest piece of fried chicken ever seen out of the final pocket.

"What is th*at*?" roared Liza with a hoot. "Fried chicken for a giant?"

"No, mon," replied Ziggy with fake dignity

as he bit into it. "It's fried turkey. Doesn't every-body eat at Kentucky Fried Turkey?"

Ziggy kept them all laughing as they finished their lunches and watched him gobble that amaz-ing meal. Rico, Rashawn, and Jerome were used to Ziggy's unusual eating habits, but the girls couldn't believe it as Ziggy bit into the grapefruit, skin and all.

After the quick lunch cleanup, the girls wan-dered down to the lake. Liza took off her shoes and socks and squealed as the chilly water touched her feet. Brandy sat on the rocky beach, writing in her notebook. Portia tossed stones into the water, trying to count the ripples and circles as they wobbled on the water. Tiana glanced over at the four boys to see what Rashawn was doing, but he was busy wrestling with Ziggy in the tall grass. She noticed a small canoe hidden under some bushes near the water's edge.

Noni tidied up the camp site, and sat down to rest a bit. She loved her job; every weekend she took small groups of children to the woods and let them explore and discover the beauty of nature.

The other side of the park was crowded with visitors who camped out with motor homes and campers, and packed the large, sandy beach of Lake Caesar. But this was real camping, she thought to herself. This was a special program—other park visitors weren't allowed in this isolated part of the park, nor could they use open fires in their campsites.

She chuckled at the four boys who were pretending to be Indian braves on a hunt. They shot imaginary arrows from invisible bows, running through the tall grasses of the meadow, darting into the shadows of the trees to hide.

"I got that moose, mon!" shouted Ziggy.

"Moose?" laughed Jerome. "Why not a squirrel or a rabbit?"

"When Ziggy hunts, he hunts moose, mon!"

Rico was on his knees, digging in the soft soil of the meadow. "Look at this funny rock, Rashawn. It's pointed, and it's such a weird color."

Rashawn looked up from where he had been sitting under a tall pine tree, pretending not to watch the girls by the water. "Let me see it." The rock was dirty, but was very light in color. "Let's take it down to the water and rinse it off."

"I'll race you!" yelled Rico as he sprinted across the meadow. Rashawn's long legs soon caught and passed Rico. Jerome and Ziggy raced also, but Jerome won easily because Ziggy's purple coat got wrapped around his legs and slowed him down.

Rico took the rock down to the water's edge and carefully washed it off. He rubbed the dirt with his fingers and with the soft sticks he found near him. His heart began to beat faster. "I think I've found something really cool," he whispered with excitement.

No one heard him because Rashawn had dumped a handful of cold lake water down Tiana's back and she screamed and ran down the small, rocky beach. Portia and Brandy had grabbed Jerome and were trying to pull him into the water. He was strong enough to laugh them off, but when Liza headed over to join them, he broke free of the girls and ran laughing in the other direction.

Rico called to Ziggy, who was running towards the girls. "Look, Ziggy—what do you think this is?"

Ziggy took the small clean stone from Rico's hand. But it wasn't a rock. It was clear like a crystal—he could see the palm of his hand beneath it. It was shaped like a small pine tree, sharply pointed, with sharp edges on each side.

"Hey, mon," whispered Ziggy with respect. I think you have found a real live Indian arrowhead!"

CHAPTER 5

"Let's go see if we can find some more arrow heads!" Rico said suddenly. He and Ziggy ran over to the spot where Rico had been digging. They dug furiously with their fingers and hands in the soft, black dirt, but all they found were dirty old rocks and worms.

"Who do you think it belonged to?" Rico asked as he wiped the dirt off his hands and looked down at the clear, shining arrowhead.

"I think it's pretty special, mon," Ziggy replied. "Most arrowheads are made of stone or some sort of rock. This one almost looks like a crystal."

"Should we show Noni?" Rico asked.

"Let's wait, mon," Ziggy suggested. "Let's just wait a bit."

Rico agreed and put the arrowhead carefully into his pocket. They walked back down to the beach where Noni was showing the girls how to put a worm on a hook to fish.

"EEEK!" screamed Portia. "It jumped out of my hand! Now I don't have to do this."

Rico ran over and picked up the worm. "Here, Portia," he said with a grin, "I think you dropped your worm." He smashed the worm into her hand. She screamed again and threw it at him. Rico chuckled and ducked.

Liza had baited her own hooks, and stared at the water, waiting for a bite. "Sh-sh-sh!" she whispered fiercely. "You'll chase away my fish."

Ziggy and Rico called to Rashawn and Jerome, and the four boys walked down the beach a little ways from where the girls were fishing. "We got something to show you, mon," Ziggy told them.

Rico pulled the arrowhead out of his pocket and showed them.

"It's quartz," stated Jerome. "That was a very special arrowhead—used for special occasions or special people."

"How do you know so much about it?" asked Rashawn.

"I did a report in school last year on Native

Americans. I remember what I read about the arrowheads because I used to think it would be really cool to find one," Jerome explained. "What are you going to do with it?"

"I don't know yet," Rico admitted. "I have a feeling there's something very special about this." They all agreed.

"Let's ask Noni what she knows about the Native Americans who used to live here," Jerome suggested.

"Yeah, mon, and she's got to tell us about the dude named Caesar, too," added Ziggy.

"I think she knows a lot," Rico said. "Doesn't she look a little like an Indian to you?"

"Just because she's got long black hair doesn't make her Indian. She looks Black to me," commented Rashawn.

"I thought she was Chinese, mon!" Ziggy exclaimed. "What difference does it make? I'm hungry!"

By the time everyone finished fishing, the shadows of the evening were beginning to darken the skies over the lake. Portia had caught six fish—more than anybody, and she carried them proudly back to the camp with the others.

The neat pile of sticks over a circle of rocks was ready to become their camp fire. Noni said, "Come and look closely. I'm going to show you a very special method of starting a fire."

"You gonna rub two sticks together?" Rico asked.

"No, you gotta rub a stone and a flint," said Jerome with authority.

"No, that's not it," grinned Noni with a little mystery in her voice. "Are you ready? Here it is!" Tiana gasped.

Noni pulled out a book of matches.

Everybody groaned and laughed. Noni started the fire and showed them how to keep it safe. It sparkled and crackled with bright orange glow.

"Let's fry this fish now," she said as she pulled a pan out of her pack.

"We're gonna eat dead fish, mon?" asked Ziggy.

Portia laughed. "No, Ziggy," she teased.

"We're gonna eat *live* fish instead!"

"Well that's better!" Ziggy replied.

Noni just shook her head at Ziggy as she showed them how to prepare and cook the fish they had caught. The sizzling smell of frying fish made everyone realize how hungry they were. Noni added a couple of sliced potatoes and onions, and dinner was ready in no time. Cold water from their canteens topped off the meal.

"Delicious!" burped Ziggy, as he finished the last of his dinner.

"I'd never eat this at home," admitted Liza. "But it was really good."

"Thanks," Noni replied. "I'm glad you liked it. Now let's get this stuff cleaned up." Everyone pitched in—Rashawn collected the paper plates and cups and tossed them in a trash bag, Tiana gathered all of the rest of the trash. Liza and Brandy gathered more sticks and branches for the fire, and Ziggy and Rico ran down to the edge of the lake to wash the pan. Jerome followed them with the plastic forks.

"Look, mon!" cried Ziggy. "I wonder who

owns that canoe."

"I know how to paddle a canoe," Rico boasted proudly. "My dad taught me last summer when I went to visit him."

"I wish we could try it out, mon," Ziggy hinted. It looks like it's been hidden here awhile. Do you think Noni knows it's here?"

"Probably not," Jerome figured. "Look at how old it is. It hasn't been used for a very long time."

"Let's get back," Rico suggested. "We'll check it out in the morning."

Darkness was falling quickly. The fire at the campsite looked bright and inviting. The boys raced back to it as the shadows of the evening became the blackness of night.

"Gather around the fire," Noni called. "Bring your sleeping bags to sit on. "I've got a story to tell you!"

Jerome, Ziggy, and Rico sat together on Rico's bag. Portia sat next to Noni, while Liza and Brandy sat on the other side of the circle. The only space left was next to Tiana, so Rashawn plopped down beside her. She smiled with excitement. His look told the boys they better not dare tease him. Ziggy rolled on the sleeping bag, hands covering his mouth, trying not to burst out laughing.

The fire in the middle of their circle was warm and cheerful. Beyond it lay only darkness. Everyone stared at it for a few moments, watching it eat the sticks and branches with a bright red sizzle and pop.

"Tell us about Caesar," Portia whispered.

"A long time ago," Noni began quietly, "no one lived in what we know as the Ohio Valley except for Native Americans. This was their land, and they roamed from the oceans to the forests and beyond, hunting only what they needed to eat, living in harmony with the land and the animals. The air was clean, the waters were blue, and nature was respected by the people who lived in it and loved it.

"About three hundred years ago, European settlers began to arrive here. Their way of life was very different. They destroyed the forests to build houses and towns. They built large farms on which they grew crops to buy and sell. And instead of trying to live with the Native Americans, they chased them off of their own land."

"Didn't the Indians fight back?" asked Rico.

"I've seen movies about the settlers and the Indians on TV," Liza said. "Usually the settlers win."

"Yeah, I've seen movies where it seems like one bullet from a settler's gun kills about five Indians," added Rashawn.

"It was a terrible time," Noni continued. "Thousands of people died, both white and Indian. Many of the government policies about the Indians were unfair and cruel. Hatred and sorrow could be found on both sides."

"Speaking of hatred and sorrow, wasn't this about the same time that slavery started?" asked Jerome. "We learned about that last year."

"You're right," Noni sighed. "Black people from Africa were being brought here as slaves to work on the huge farms in the South."

"Why didn't they make the Indians be slaves?" Tiana asked.

"Well, they tried. But the Native Americans lived here and knew the land and forests well. They could escape and never be found because they had friends nearby who spoke their language and who could help them. Black people looked different and were easily spotted. And they had no one to help them, except . . . ."

"Except who, mon?" Ziggy asked with excitement.

Noni paused to make sure everyone was listening. The fire crackled and insects chirped in the distance.

" . . . . except the Indians!"

"Indians?" Brandy asked with surprise. "Why would they help runaway slaves?"

"They probably thought it was cool to upset the slave owners," Liza said.

"Yeah, and they probably would want to help anybody who was being mistreated even worse than they were," added Portia.

"You're both right," Noni admitted. "Thousands of runaway slaves were helped by Native Americans. But there's more!"

"So tell us, mon!" Ziggy insisted. He loved stories with secrets.

"Many of the runaways stayed with the Indians. They were accepted and adopted into the Indian tribes and became part of their families."

"Awesome!" declared Rashawn.

"How come that wasn't in the books when I did my report on Native Americans last year?" asked Jerome.

"There's quite a bit that's sometimes left out of history books," Noni admitted. "This is just another fact of history that's often overlooked."

"Yeah, like this Caesar dude, mon," added Ziggy. "If he was so great and got a park named after him, how come we never heard of him?"

"And how come you know so much about him?" Brandy asked.

"Caesar was my great-great-great grandfather," Noni said quietly.

CHAPTER 6

"Wow!" Liza exclaimed. "Why didn't you tell us?"

"You didn't ask!" Noni smiled.

"Was he a slave?" Jerome wanted to know.

"Yes. From what we know, he was a harness maker and blacksmith in Maryland. His master brought him on a trip to this area somewhere near the year 1776.

"Gee, that was the year of the start of the Revolutionary War!" Portia remembered.

"Right. Americans fought for freedom in that war, but not for freedom for slaves. It took another hundred years for that," Noni added.

"But what about Caesar, mon? Finish the story!" cried Ziggy with impatience.

"Okay, Ziggy," Noni smiled. "We're not sure, but Caesar either escaped from his owner while he was here, or another story says his owner was killed."

"I bet he saw this valley and just took off!"

said Rico, matter of factly.

"The Shawnee Indians found him hiding in the woods and took him to their village. They fed him and gave him a warm and safe place to sleep," Noni continued.

"I wonder if he was scared," Portia wondered.

"He was probably so happy to be safe and free that he didn't have time to be scared!" Liza answered.

"Caesar stayed with the Indians for several months. They taught him their language and how to find food as well as joy in the forest."

"Too bad he didn't have anything to give back to them," Jerome said.

"Oh, no, not at all!" Noni said with surprise. "In a way, Caesar saved their lives!"

"How?" asked Brandy. She was gobbling jelly beans again.

"Caesar was a harness maker. He knew how to make belts and harnesses and ropes from leather, how to connect buckles to hold them. The Indian harnesses were thin and broke easily. When they went into battle, sometimes they lost control of the horse because of the weak harness."

"They would fall off?" asked Portia.

"With a thud!" answered Noni.

"Ouch!"

"Many times the harness was so weak," Noni added with a chuckle, "the only reason the Indian didn't fall off was because the horse liked him!"

"I bet I could ride a horse bareback!" boasted Rico.

"And I bet he'd throw you on your bare back, mon!" laughed Ziggy.

Noni continued, "Anyway, Caesar taught the Indians how to make tight leather harnesses with buckles for their horses. It really made a difference. In addition, he was wise and kind and they loved him for his gentle spirit."

"So that's why the Shawnees gave him the land?" asked Liza.

"Yes, they first found him by a creek that they named Caesar's Creek. And when they gave him this valley as a token of their appreciation for him, hundreds and hundreds of beautiful acres, this whole area became known as the Caesar Creek area."

"I thought you said he was an Indian chief," declared Rashawn.

"Yes, he was!" Noni replied with pride. He stayed with the Shawnee for the rest of his life. He married a Shawnee woman and had several children. Later, he was placed in charge of several other families and rose to the rank of sub-chief, second only to the principal chief of the tribe!"

"Wow!"

"Do you think he could make arrowheads?" Rico asked.

"Sure, Rico," Noni answered. "He probably used quartz tips, since he was a chief. Why do you ask?"

Rico and Ziggy looked at each other and grinned. "Oh, no special reason," Rico said quickly. "Do you think there are any arrowheads around here? It would be cool to find one."

"It's probably possible to find flint arrowheads, but quartz tips are very rare and special,"

Noni replied. "Indian boys about your age were taught to make tips for their arrows by the older men of the tribe."

"What was it like for Indian kids our age?" Jerome asked.

"All of the children were loved and adored. Every adult in the tribe helped care for and discipline the children, so it was like one big family."

"Did the girls have to do dumb stuff like sewing and cooking?" asked Liza.

"The women and girls usually took care of making the clothes and preparing the food, yes, but they also had power in the tribal council and could even be chief."

"Well, I guess that makes me feel a little better," Liza said. "But how come girls couldn't go hunting for game?"

"Oh, they did. Many of the women were expert marksmen—some could even out-shoot the men," Noni informed her.

"Cool!"

"What about the boys?" asked Rico. "They always get to do mighty deeds to prove their courage and stuff!"

"You're right, Rico," Noni began, "the boys did have manhood ceremonies. Really cool stuff."

Ziggy stood up and raised his fists like a warrior. "That's me, mon! Cool Indian brave!"

The girls just stared at him, making faces of disgust. Noni smiled half hearted at the stereotype and whispered to Liza and Brandy, "Watch this!"

"Okay, Ziggy," Noni called, "would you like to demonstrate one of the Shawnee ceremonies that boys did to prove their manhood?"

"Yeah, mon!" Ziggy jumped and danced around the fire copying movies he had seen on TV.

Noni explained, "Every boy in the tribe, at the age of eight or nine, had to take a walk every morning."

"I can do that!" Ziggy declared. "No problem, mon!"

"They had to walk to the river."

"No problem!"

"Every morning for three months."

"No problem!"

"Did I mention the three months were December, January, and February?"

"No problem! I'd wear a coat!"

"Did I mention that at the end of the walk, the boy had to jump in the river?"

"No problem, mon! Uh, wouldn't my shoes and coat get wet?"

Noni was about to pop with laughter. "Did I mention that the boy took this walk every morning in the snow with no shoes?"

"No prob—. Uh, no shoes?"

"Did I mention that the boy took this walk every morning and then jumped into the frozen river with *no clothes on*?"

"No way, mon!" Ziggy sat back down in a hurry and shivered. The girls were rolling with laughter.

"Really cool manhood stuff, Ziggy!" teased Tiana. "So cool you'd be frozen!"

Noni laughed, too. "You know, people still talk about when the great Shawnee warrior, Tecumseh, was a boy, and how he had to do his challenge in the snow."

"I heard about Tecumseh!" said Brandy with excitement. "We read about him in school. What did he do for his challenge?

"Tecumseh walked naked in the snow in the coldest winter ever known; the water was frozen most mornings and had to be broken for him so he could jump in."

"Ouch! Maybe I'm not ready to be a warrior just yet, mon," Ziggy admitted. "Were they any easier tests?" he asked with a grin.

"There were other manhood tests as well, and special challenges for the young girls also," Noni answered. "The young people would have to go on trips alone, sometimes in the woods at night, sometimes on the water, sometimes in the Great House, which was their place of the spirit."

"Look at the moon," Brandy said suddenly. Above, the moon was bright and golden—a full moon. It shone on the dark still water of the lake in the distance, shimmering like candle light.

"A mystery moon," murmured Noni in a whisper. "Strange events will happen tonight! Shadows walk in the moonlight."

CHAPTER 7

"What do you mean, 'strange events'?" asked Portia. She looked up at the moon and back into the flames of the sparkling fire.

"And what kind of shadows will walk?" added Brandy. Tiana shivered and moved a fraction closer to Rashawn.

Noni's face looked dark and mysterious. Her voice was low and scary as she whispered again, "Shadows walk in the moonlight!"

"You mean like ghosts?" asked Rico.

"You trying to scare us, mon?" Ziggy asked. "Cause you might be doing a good job!"

"There are spirits everywhere," Noni continued mysteriously. "Spirits of the past and spirits of hope and spirits of those who once walked this land. Are you brave enough to sleep in the darkness with the shadows of the past?"

"You can't scare us!" boasted Rashawn. "We're ready to go to sleep without any flashlights, even!"

"No problem, mon!" Ziggy added.

Jerome said boldly, "Bring on all your ghosts and shadows and spirits. "We're the Black Dinosaurs! We ain't scared of nothing!"

Rico joined them as they stood and marched to their tent, but he looked scared. They could hear Noni and the girls laughing behind them.

"Dumb girls!" Rico said. "They got Noni to protect them, though."

"We don't need anybody, mon," Ziggy boasted. "She was just trying to scare us. That's what you're supposed to do to kids on a camp out!"

They crawled into their sleeping bags, which fit snugly into the tent. Each boy had a flashlight. "Ready to zip the tent?" Jerome asked.

"Ready, mon!"

"Let her zip!" added Rico.

"Now, flashlights off!" commanded Rashawn.

The darkness was almost total. They could see faint shadows from the light of the moon above.

"You scared?" asked Rico.

"Not really," admitted Rashawn.

"Me neither," said Jerome. "I just hope there's no bugs crawling around inside this sleeping bag!"

"Where's the arrowhead, Rico?" Ziggy asked.

"Right here in my pocket. You know," he added, "I wish we could do one of those manhood tests Noni talked about."

"Like jumping naked in a frozen lake, mon? You must be nuts!"

"No, I mean like going on a night hike or searching for secrets in the stars.

"We could go on a hike tonight," Rashawn suggested quietly.

"Noni would never allow it," Rico declared.

"Noni would never know!" Rashawn replied with excitement in his voice. "We'll wait until she's asleep."

"You mean sneak out, mon? Awesome!"

"We'll get in really big trouble!"

"Only if we get caught!"

"How could they catch us? We'll be back in an hour!"

"Let's prove we're men, and not boys!"

"It's dark!"

"We've got flashlights."

"What about the bugs?"

"We'll take bug spray."

"Let's do it!"

"Yeah, mon! Let's do it!"

They whispered with excitement for the next hour, listening for the sounds from the girls' tent to disappear. The plan was to walk down to the beach by the lake and sit in the moonlight, pretending to be a Shawnee boy on a night journey. If Noni woke up and found them, they decided to tell her they had come out to go to the bathroom.

The night finally became silent. Rashawn unzipped the tent and listened. They could hear insects and frogs, but the tent of Noni and the girls was quiet. They waited another half an hour, just to make sure, then slipped quietly, one by one, out of the tent and down the path to the lake.

The night air was chilly and Rashawn wished he had taken his mother's advice and brought his coat. The moon glowed huge and bright, lighting the water. As the four boys sat on the banks of Lake Caesar, they thought silently of Indians, and adventures, and secrets of the past.

"This is cool!" Rashawn sighed.

"Awesome!" added Jerome.

Ziggy wore his long, purple, many-pocketed coat. He and Rico walked down the beach, scuffing their shoes in the rocky sand, and almost bumped into the canoe they had discovered earlier.

"Look, mon!" Ziggy exclaimed.

"I wonder if it's any good," Rico wondered. "It's probably full of holes." They called Jerome and Rashawn over to help them inspect the hull of the canoe. They shone their flashlights all over it and it looked faded, but surprisingly solid.

Together they pushed it and pulled it over. It was about fifteen feet long. Two seats had been nailed across it, and two oars were tucked neatly on each side. Inside the boat was a flat wooden board. Hand-lettered on this plank, in faded white paint, were the words, "BOAT FOR SALE".

"It looks like it's been waiting for us, mon,"

Ziggy remarked with excitement. He climbed in.

"Maybe we better not," Rico warned.

"What harm could there be?" Rashawn said. "We're only gonna sit here on the beach for a minute." He climbed in next to Ziggy.

Jerome got in next. "Come on, Rico!" he called.

Rico climbed in next to Jerome, grinning in spite of himself.

"Indian scouts, out looking for trouble!" Jerome announced. They unhooked the oars and pretended to paddle the boat as they checked for enemies in the distance.

"Let's see if it floats," Rashawn said suddenly. He jumped out of the canoe. The other boys jumped out, too, excited because they had all had the same thought. "Come on, help me push it into the water!"

Rico didn't want to, but he helped anyway. With a huge push from the boys, the canoe slipped silently into the black water of Lake Caesar and started to float away from the shore.

"Catch it!" shouted Jerome. "If it floats away,

we'll get in trouble!" He ran into the water and reached for the canoe, but he couldn't hold it alone.

"Jump in, mon!" yelled Ziggy. Rashawn grabbed for the other side and pulled himself into the bottom of the boat.

Ziggy jumped in next. Finally Rico, who didn't want the other boys to tease him, jumped in as well. The four boys looked around.

The boat had drifted thirty feet from the shore. Slightly wet and really excited, the boys grinned with pleasure as the small canoe rocked gently in the night breeze, drifting away with each rock of the waves. The moon still shone brightly, lighting what looked like a path on the water.

"I feel like a Shawnee boy!" Rashawn said with a smile.

"On a night challenge?

"Maybe, but this is pretty easy," Rashawn boasted.

"We better get back, mon!" Ziggy suggested with regret. Rico was glad that someone else had said what he'd been thinking.

"Where are the oars?" asked Rico.

"Uh-oh! I think we've got a small problem— no, make that BIG problem," Jerome said quietly.

"What's wrong?"

"We left the oars on shore!"

CHAPTER 8

The breeze had picked up, and as they looked back at the beach, they saw that the canoe had drifted almost a hundred feet from the shore. They could see in the distance what looked like the tiny faint glow of their campfire. All around them rippled the dark, silent water.

"What are we gonna do?" Rico worried. "I knew this wasn't a good idea!

"We can't swim back to shore," said Jerome. "It's too dark and the water is too deep."

"What if we call for help?" Rashawn suggested.

"Who's gonna hear us, mon?" Ziggy moaned. "Now I really do have to go to the bathroom!"

The canoe bounced on the water, drifting the four friends farther and farther away from camp, and safety, and even the girls.

"Do you think Noni will get up and check on us?" Jerome asked.

"Yeah, mon, but even if she does, where will she look for us in the middle of the night?" Ziggy answered with defeat.

"Maybe she knows about the canoe and will notice that it's gone, mon. Not to worry—not to worry!" Ziggy repeated, but he sounded worried anyway.

"And maybe she won't notice at all," moaned Rico. "We may drift here all night!"

"What would Tecumseh do?" asked Jerome. "If this was a night challenge, a young person would have to be brave and think of a solution, right?"

"Right," agreed Rashawn. "But I don't feel very brave. I'm cold and I wish I had listened to my mother and brought my coat.

"Hey, I got an idea, mon!" Ziggy said suddenly. "What about this 'BOAT FOR SALE' sign? We could use it as an oar!"

"Good idea, Ziggy!" said Jerome. "Rico, you said you knew how to paddle with an oar. Do your thing, man!"

Rico picked up the plank and dipped it slowly into the water. He pulled it through the water as his father had shown him. But the canoe barely moved.

"What's wrong, Rico?" Why aren't we moving?" Rashawn asked.

"When I was with my dad, it was much easier," admitted Rico. "And it was daytime. And he was doing most of the paddling."

"Let's take turns, then," suggested Jerome. "Let me try."

Jerome tried paddling with the plank and agreed that it was much harder than it looked. The little canoe bobbed on the water, turning and moving a little as each boy took a turn, but it was no closer to the shore. They could no longer see even a dim spot of their camp fire, and the moon had disappeared behind the clouds. Blackness surrounded them.

"We're lost."

"In the dark."

"In the middle of a lake."

"In the middle of the night."

"Not to worry, mon!" Ziggy said suddenly. "I have an idea!"

Ziggy started digging though the many pockets of his purple coat. "I know it's in here somewhere," he mumbled. Finally he said with a shout of joy, "I found it!"

"What?" they all wanted to know.

"My umbrella, of course!" He showed them a tiny two-tone green umbrella, which, folded up, was only about five inches long.

"What good is that going to do?" asked Rashawn. It's not raining."

"I know, mon. But look!" Ziggy pushed a button on the handle and the tiny umbrella stretched out to a full three feet long. "We can use this as a second oar! As long as I don't push this second button to open it up, we'll be fine," he explained.

Ziggy dipped the umbrella into the water and said to Rico, who had the plank-oar, "Let's do this together, mon. Dip, push the water, up—dip, push the water, up—dip, push up—dip, push up."

Rico grinned in agreement, and for a few moments the sound of the two make-shift oars splashing together in the water made them all feel better. But the canoe still wasn't moving towards the shore as they wanted. In fact, it seemed to be going in circles.

"It's not working, Ziggy," Jerome complained.

"I've got it, mon!" Ziggy said with excitement. "The problem is that me and Rico should be sitting next to each other, not like this! That way, we'd be rowing together and we could get this little boat back to camp. Let me just move over next to . . . ."

"NO, ZIGGY!" they all shouted. "DON'T STAND UP!"

But it was too late. In his excitement to change places, he stood up, and the canoe started to rock. Ziggy lost his balance, fell forward, and accidentally pushed the button which made the umbrella open with a WHOOSH! The open umbrella bumped Rashawn and knocked him overboard with a splash. Ziggy tumbled in after him, screaming. He grabbed the side of the canoe, pulled it too far, and Rico and Jerome joined them in the chilly water as the canoe tilted, filled with water, and sank with a gurgle and a thud.

The four boys were good swimmers, but the darkness and the sudden tumble into the water made everything really scary. Ziggy was screaming and splashing, trying to find the sunken canoe.

"Help! I'm drowning! It's dark out here! Where are you guys?"

"We're right here, Ziggy! Grab my hand!" Jerome shouted.

"I can't find you, mon!" The water is much too deep! I can't swim in the dark, mon! Help!"

Finally Rashawn yelled, "ZIGGY! SHUT UP AND STAND UP!" We're in three feet of water! Look!"

Silence.

Then Ziggy said quietly, "I knew that, mon. I was just trying to see if you had noticed." He stood up and sloshed through the shallow water to the shore.

Rico, Rashawn, and Jerome laughed in spite of themselves and followed him. Wet and cold, but glad to be safe, they sat on the sand, trying to catch their breath. "We made it!" sighed Rico.

"Let's brush this sand off and head back to

camp in a hurry!" said Jerome. "Maybe Noni hasn't noticed we were gone yet."

"Sand?" Rashawn said with worry in his voice. He picked up handfuls of the soft white sand and let it spill through his fingers. Then he said with quiet fear, "There was no sand on the beach we left from. It was rocky, remember?"

"Oh, no!" groaned Rico. "We've landed on another beach! We must have drifted across the lake! Now we'll never find our way back!"

"Well, we can't stay here. We've got to keep moving so we can dry off a little and try to keep warm," declared Jerome. "Maybe our camp is not too far away." But he didn't sound too sure.

"Let's go this way," suggested Rico.

"Through the woods?" asked Rashawn.

"Why not, mon! Let's move on!" Ziggy led their way into the darkness.

They walked slowly at first, stumbling into trees and each other, bushes scratching their arms and faces. Gradually, though, the moon came from behind the clouds and they were able to make out shapes and shadows in the forest as they walked.

But they were wet, cold, scared, and very, very lost.

"I wish I had a flashlight," Jerome sighed out loud.

"As long as we're wishing, mon, wish for dry clothes and a pizza!" Ziggy added.

"I wish we were back home," Rico said quietly.

"You can't have an adventure at home, Rico! Think of this as our manhood ceremony, like the Shawnee boys," Rashawn explained as he stumbled over a vine. "The spirits of Caesar and Tecumseh are watching us. They expect us to be brave."

"I'd rather be brave in the daytime," Rico sighed.

They came to a clearing. A huge log lay across one edge of this break in the thick woods. A large flat rock lay close by. Faint moonlight shone through the trees. Ziggy, Jerome, and Rico sat on the log. Rashawn stretched out on the rock. Jerome scratched his mosquito bites, and checked the area for bugs as best he could in the darkness.

"Wish I had some bug spray, too," he whispered to himself.

"What should we do?" asked Rico.

"Well, we can't stay here. We've got to find our way out of here!" Jerome replied. "The lake is a big circle. We just walk around it until we find our camp!"

"It's a big lake," reminded Rashawn. "And we don't even know whether to go left or right."

"I saw a movie about some kids who were lost in the woods for six weeks," Rico remembered.

"So what happened in the movie?"

"The kids ate bugs and worms and leaves and stuff, until they got rescued!"

"Yucky, mon! No bugs or worms for Ziggy! Let's get out of here!"

"What would Tecumseh have done in this situation?" asked Rico quietly. A owl hooted above him and he jumped.

"Tecumseh would not be lost. He'd know these woods like we know the mall," Jerome replied.

"I know he wouldn't be scared. He would know to use his head and find his way," added Rashawn.

"He'd be scared if he knew he would get in trouble when he got back, like we will, mon," Ziggy reminded them. "Noni is gonna kill us!"

"If a bear doesn't kill us first!" exclaimed Rico. What was that?" They all heard the rustling noise behind them.

"What was that?" whispered Jerome.

"A rabbit, maybe?" said Rico hopefully.

"Or the bear, mon!" whispered Ziggy with excitement and mystery in his voice.

They heard it again, louder this time, and closer. They could hear it moving through the crunchy leaves. It seemed to be running right toward them!

"Maybe it's a lion or tiger!" Jerome joked weakly.

"That's not funny!" Rico shouted as they started to run away from the noise.

"No, mon, I think it really IS a bear! But whatever it is, here it comes!" Ziggy screamed.

The four terrified boys yelled and screamed in fear and started running wildly into the night.

CHAPTER 9

Terrified of the huge black bear that surely was following them, the four boys ran wildly through the woods. Ziggy, usually the slowest because he liked to act silly, was in front this time. The breeze of the evening chilled his wet, sticky clothes, which stuck to his body as he ran, but he didn't even notice. Rico, close behind Ziggy, tripped over a small branch and fell forward, knocking Ziggy even further ahead of him in the darkness.

Ziggy yelled over his shoulder, "You all right, mon?"

Gasping for breath, Rico panted, "Yeah, I'm okay, just keep running! I think it's getting closer!

Jerome and Rashawn, just a little behind Rico yelled ahead, "We can hear the bear! It's gonna get us! Run!"

Rico yelled to the others, "Find a tree and climb it! It's our only hope of escape!"

With large, gasping breaths, Ziggy replied, "Don't you know that bears can climb trees too, mon? Just run!"

Jerome knew that bugs were biting his bare legs, which were cut and scratched from the bushes and briars. He wanted to scratch, but didn't dare. "I wish I knew where the camp was!" he moaned as he ran.

"We're good and lost!" gasped Jerome. "Plus I think we're going to be dinner for that bear!"

The noise in the bushes behind them got louder and closer. The animal had tracked them and was only a few feet behind them. It was just a matter of time.

Ziggy broke a speed record. He ignored branches and scratches and even his fear of the darkness. He didn't know where he was heading anymore. He was lost, and afraid, and out of breath. In the moonlight, he could see the shadows of the trees ahead. He ran for the tree straight in front of him, hoping to try to climb it, hoping this bear didn't know it was supposed to be able to climb up after him.

Suddenly, the tree moved! Standing straight and tall in front of him now were the shadows of two trees—and one of them was moving toward him.

Ziggy screamed and tried to turn, but the branches of the tall shadow tree reached out and grabbed his wrist. Then the tree spoke to him in a powerful voice. "Where are you going in such a hurry in the middle of the night?"

By this time Rico, Rashawn, and Jerome had reached Ziggy and stopped, panting and gasping, almost too tired to scream. "Help!" breathed Rico. "A bear is chasing us!"

The shadows of the clouds moved from the moon and for a moment, the boys could see clearly. It was not a tree that held the trembling Ziggy, but a man, tall and strong. "I see no bear," he said quietly. "And all I hear is the silence of the night, that is, now that you young men are quiet. Even my ancestors could hear all that noise you were making from miles away," he chuckled.

The four friends looked at each other in amazement. The night was dark, the breeze was cool, and all was silent except for the forest voices of the night.

"Who are you?" Jerome wanted to know as the man gently released Ziggy and set him on a bed of soft leaves.

"Can you get us back to our camp?" asked Rico, who was worried that they would get in trouble.

"Where are we?" Now that the immediate danger seemed to be over, and Rashawn had started breathing normally again, he was ready to find out.

"What happened to the bear, mon?" Ziggy asked finally. At that moment, a large raccoon waddled slowly into the clearing. It glanced at the strange group that was disturbing its night, and moved on into the forest.

"Our bear was a raccoon?" Rico said in disbelief. If I wasn't so scared, that would be funny!"

"Maybe it was *makwa*, the bear, my young friend, and maybe not. Perhaps because of your fear of the darkness and your lack of knowledge about the forest, the night spirits let you *think* you heard a bear. Perhaps it was only your own fear that was chasing you."

"Could be, mon," replied Ziggy thoughtfully. "We were pretty scared. We've been lost for a long time, and we got separated in the woods. We might have been running from each other!"

"Can you help us get back? We're on a camp out with our school," asked Rico, who worried enough for the four of them.

"I know that campground; it is on the other side of the lake. How did you get here?" the stranger asked.

"We took a canoe. We wanted to try a night challenge—like Indian boys. At first it was fun, but then the canoe started floating away, so we jumped in, and then we couldn't get back because all we had for oars were a board and an umbrella, then our canoe turned over, and we got all wet, and we were really lost, and then we got scared, and started running—and we ran into you!" explained Rico all in one breath.

"You never told us who you were, mon," said Ziggy quietly.

The stranger smiled. "My name is Hawk. Come, young friends. Let me give you food and rest. The journey back is long without a canoe, and *Keelswah,* the morning sun, will soon erase the shadows of the night. I will take you safely back to your camp."

They followed the tall, quiet stranger down a path of soft pine needles to a small lean-to built of branches and bark. It stood close to a rock wall. A small fire burned quietly, barely disturbing the darkness; the smell of a savory soup greeted the boys who suddenly realized just how tired and hungry they really were. From a leather bag Hawk brought out four clay bowls, which he filled with the soup and handed to each boy. He had two blankets, so he put one around Rico and Rashawn, and one around Jerome and Ziggy.

Hawk sat on a log, chuckling, watching the four boys drink the warm soup with satisfaction. He knew that the appetite of the young was deep as a valley, so he refilled their bowls several times. He then showed them how to rinse their bowls in the stream that the boys had not even noticed, and they drank the cold, sweet water until they were filled.

Ziggy burped and everyone laughed. "Excuse me, mon," said Ziggy, cheerful once again. "That was a delicious meal. Even my mum couldn't beat that! Many thanks! My name is Ziggy!"

"And I'm Rico. You're a good cook. Thanks for the blankets, too. Are we far from our camp?"

"My name is Jerome," added Jerome as he offered his hand to Hawk. "Thanks for saving us."

"My name is Rashawn. You saved our lives! Do you live in these woods?"

"I only saved you from the shadows. The sunlight would have made your journey less frightening. And no, I don't live here. I love these woods—sometimes I need to feel close to the earth and I walk and camp alone for a day or two."

"Are you an Indian, mon?" Ziggy finally blurted out.

"Yes, I am," Hawk replied with quiet dignity. "I am Shawnee."

"You couldn't be! You wear glasses! Indians don't wear glasses!" argued Rico.

Hawk chuckled. "Sorry to disappoint you."

Jerome said quietly, "When I did my report on Native Americans last year, my history book said there that there were no more Shawnee Indians left in Ohio! I remember, because I wondered what had happened."

"History books do not always speak the truth, my son," said Hawk with a sigh. "There is much that is not said as well. Let me tell you a story."

Jerome and Rashawn sat cross-legged on the soft pine-needle floor of the lean-to, their backs against the warm stone wall. Rico and Ziggy sat close to the fire, intent on the bright, piercing eyes and wise, warm face of Hawk. Hawk's hair, which was black mixed with gray, was long and tied back with a leather string. He wore dark jeans, a brown shirt, and glasses. Around his neck was a leather thong from which hung a small leather pouch. Hawk's voice was low, but strong as he began his tale.

"My name is Tukemas Pope and I am chief

of the Shawnee Nation of Ohio, United Remnant Band. My friends call me Hawk. We are all that is left here in Ohio of the millions of Shawnee who once called this land home. Our tribal lands are at a place called Shawandasse, which is not very far from here. The word *Shawandasse* means 'South Wind people.' "

"Wow! You're a chief? Should we call you 'Your Majesty'?" asked Rico.

"Goodness, no!" laughed Hawk. "Just call me Hawk."

"What happened to the millions of Shawnee you talked about?" Rashawn asked.

"Some were killed, some died of disease and starvation, and many died as they were forced to move from Ohio to other states. It was a very sad time for our people," Hawk replied with emotion.

"That's awful!" cried Jerome. "Are there many Indians left in Ohio?" asked Jerome.

"You're supposed to say 'Native Americans,' not Indians," corrected Rico. "Isn't that right, Hawk?"

"Actually, both are acceptable," Hawk

explained. We were named Indians by an explorer who thought, when he reached America, that he had reached India! Boy, was he mixed up! But the name has stuck. As long as you don't use the word in a negative way, and remember that we are the native people of this country, then 'Indian' is usually okay."

"I see," said Rashawn, "kinda like Black and African-American."

"Yes, a little," replied Hawk.

"Are you the chief of a big tribe?" asked Jerome.

"We have over six hundred in our band here in Ohio, and there are other Shawnee in other states, but there are hundreds of thousands of native people living all over this country, on reservations, in small towns, in big cities—everywhere. We are part of the American fabric just like you."

"Hey Hawk-mon! Have you ever heard of Tecumseh?" asked Ziggy. He was an Indian from Ohio. We learned about him in school."

"And what about Caesar?" added Rashawn. We just found out that this park was named for a

Black man who lived with the Shawnee. You know anything about him?"

"Tecumseh was not just 'an Indian from Ohio.'" Hawk replied with fire in his eyes. He was the greatest Shawnee warrior ever to walk these lands, a hero to all generations.

"And yes, I know the story of Caesar as well. Tecumseh and Caesar were friends. Native Americans and African Americans shared much in years past. So much of that has been hidden by the shadows of time. Listen, and I will share with you the secrets and shadows of Caesar's Creek!"

CHAPTER 10

"Did Caesar have to do manhood ceremonies like Tecumseh?" Rico wanted to know. "Our camp counselor told us about the winter challenge."

"Caesar might have had to prove his manhood when he was accepted into the tribe, but only boys got to do the winter ordeal," Hawk replied.

"Our counselor Noni told us she was the great-great-great granddaughter of Caesar. Are you any relation to Tecumseh?" asked Jerome.

"No, son. But my spirit relates to him." Hawk paused for a moment. "Even as a child, Tecumseh was special. The night he was born, a great meteor streaked through the sky. It was a very special sign."

"You mean he didn't get cold when he jumped in that frozen water, mon?" Ziggy asked.

"Of course he was cold, but he had to learn to find the fire within himself and not feel the cold and the snow and the ice," Hawk explained.

"Wow! He was tougher than I could ever be," admitted Jerome. "I bet he ran back to his house when he got out of that frozen water!"

"Oh no!" Hawk cried. "Tecumseh walked back slowly and with dignity, as did his father before him," Hawk said with a proud smile.

"Were they glad to get to the last day of that ordeal?" asked Rashawn.

"Well, yes and no," Hawk replied. "On the last day of their three-month challenge, the boys had to jump into the frozen water four times. On the last jump, they had to go down to the bottom, and bring back whatever they put their hands on. Sometimes they would bring up grass, or dirt, or rocks; everyone once in a while, a boy would bring up something really special."

"What did Tecumseh find, mon?" Ziggy asked with excitement.

"It was a stone—but not just any stone. It glowed with different colors, and changed as light shined on it. Sometimes it looked like the eye of Peshewa, the panther; sometimes like a star from the sky. It was very unusual and very special. And so was he."

"Awesome," whispered Rashawn.

"So how did Caesar know Tecumseh?" Jerome asked.

"Caesar came to the Shawnee when Tecumseh was about eight years old, probably right around the time of his winter manhood challenge, so he would have been one of the elders who helped Tecumseh grow to be the great man that he became."

The fire crackled and Ziggy shivered as he glanced at the moon, which was fading as morning grew near. He thought of what Noni had said. "She was right, mon" he thought to himself. "A mystery moon," Noni had whispered. "Strange events will happen tonight! Shadows will walk in the moon-light."

"It's almost morning," Rico said. "Then, re-membering the arrowhead he had found, he took it out of his pocket, and gave it to Hawk. "We found this," he explained. "But I want you to have it. Maybe it belonged to Tecumseh or Caesar."

Hawk smiled as he glanced at the arrowhead. "This is very special, and I thank you for the gift. Perhaps it did once belong to one of the great ones. But I want you boys to keep it as my gift, as a memory of this night. Life must give to life," he said quietly.

"Thanks, Hawk," Rico said with feeling.

"Can you show us how to get back to our camp, Hawk?" Jerome asked. "This has been an amazing night, but we're gonna get killed if we don't get back!"

"Well, it looks like you boys got your night challenge anyway," chuckled Hawk. "Let's head out of here, young braves!"

They were still a little damp, and really tired, but the four boys were ready to go. A little stiff, but smiling, they followed Hawk into the woods. The miles seemed to pass quickly as Hawk told them stories that his people had told to children for generations. Gradually, the darkness faded and the shadows of the night were replaced by sunshine.

Ziggy's cheerful mood had returned with the return of daylight, and he laughed at the birds and squirrels as he jogged on the trail beside Hawk and the other boys.

"Look, mon!" he cried, as he picked up a bright red rock, then an orange one, then a purple one. "They look like . . . ."

"They're not rocks!" cried Rico. "They're

jellybeans! Brandy's jellybeans! We're almost there!"

Hawk grinned, proud that they were able to find the trail on their own. Soon, once again the path had widened, and the trees disappeared behind them. They stood once again on the edge of the huge meadow, which still shone with a golden glow. On the other side of the meadow lay a large blue lake, the lake that had terrified them just a few hours before. To their left stood the two small tents, and the remains of their fire. Noni and the girls ran towards them.

"Where have you been?!!" Noni yelled with relief and anger. "We thought you were lost or hurt or worse!"

"We've been looking for you since before daylight!" Portia reported.

"You're gonna get it!" warned Liza.

"Did you take that canoe out?" whispered Tiana to Rashawn. He nodded and smiled.

"It was fun at first. I'll tell you all about it later," he whispered back.

The boys introduced Hawk and tried to

explain everything that had happened all at the same time. Once Noni understood that they were safe, she relaxed, but they knew they were still in big trouble.

Hawk said to her, "Don't be too hard on the young braves here. They did wrong, we know, but they passed their challenge like men. I'm very proud to know them."

Ziggy grinned with pride. "Thanks, mon. I have a gift for you, something I want you to have."

Rico, Rashawn, and Jerome shook Hawk's hand and thanked him once again. He hugged them and told them he must go.

Hawk stooped down and gathered all eight children around him. "Come, my children," he said. "Remember the songs of the wind and the trees. Remember the secrets of the shadows. Life must give to life. Tanakia . . . Farewell."

"Tanakia, mon," said Ziggy softly. "Bye."

Hawk turned to wave good-bye as he walked back into the woods. Noni and the children waved, calling their thanks to the tall, smiling Shawnee who proudly wore a slightly damp, many-pocketed, long purple coat.

About the Author

If you were to ask Sharon M. Draper how often she writes, her answer would probably be, "whenever I get the chance."

Born in Cleveland, Ohio, Sharon M. Draper is a professional educator as well as an accomplished writer. She has spent more than twenty-five years teaching junior and senior high school students how to communicate their ideas effectively. A graduate of Pepperdine University, Sharon Mills Draper 's literary recognition began when she won first prize in the Gertrude H. Johnson Williams Literary Contest and had her short story, "One Small Torch" published in *Ebony* magazine. She was also recipient of the first Genesis Award for her YA novel, *Tears of A Tiger*. It was presented by the Coretta Scott King Award Committee of the American Library Association to recognize work of literary merit by a new writer.

Ms. Draper was named the National Teacher of the Year in 1997. She travels extensively and is an accomplished public speaker who addresses educational and literary groups of all ages. She lives in Cincinnati, Ohio with her husband and four children and is working on several additional adventure stories for the Ziggy and The Black Dinosaurs™ series, which is fast becoming a favorite for middle readers all over the country.

Authors Note:

Caesar and Tecumseh were real people who lived in Ohio long ago. Hawk Pope is a real person who lives in Ohio today. He is the chief of the Shawnee in Ohio, United Remnant Band. All the other characters in the story, *Ziggy and The Black Dinosaurs™: Shadows of Caesar's Creek*, are fictional. Caesar has many descendants who still live in Ohio, but Noni is a fictional character.

Caesar's history mapped

State park named for frontier explorer
by Randy McNutt
THE CINCINNATI ENQUIRER

The following article is reprinted by permission of the *Cincinnati Enquirer* (July 16, 1996). It was originaly published July 16, 1996.

WAYNESVILLE—For 20 years, Dennis Dalton has tracked him—through libraries, country cemeteries and the back pages of history.

Today, Mr. Dalton will discuss the life of Caesar, namesake of Caesar Creek State Park, with descendants of the frontier explorer and runaway slave.

"It has taken a lot of time and effort to uncover the genealogy," said Nancy Caesar Donaldson, 65, of Dayton, who thinks she is Caesar's great-great-great-granddaughter.

She hopes that 50 to 100 Caesars will attend the private reunion, from noon to 5 p.m. today at Pioneer Village near the state park.

"When we were young, people used to tease us about the name Caesar." She said. "Then about 10 years ago, somebody told me about a black man named Caesar, and how the state had named a park after him. So I started researching, trying to connect him to us. Then Dennis contacted me." Mr. Dalton, 52, Waynesville's historian and writer of

the park's local history, has been studying Caesar and regional history since childhood.

"Caesar had only one name, so it was difficult to trace his descendants," Mr. Dalton said. "I knew that about 1,800 classical slave names like his were changed to regular names. That made things easier. Caesar became a last name."

Mr. Dalton called Caesar's he found in Dayton and North Carolina. At the same time, Mrs. Donaldson conducted her own research.

"We have struggle with this for a long time," she said.

Although Mrs. Donaldson cannot say conclusively that her family is related to Caesar, she and Mr. Dalton are convinced.

"Unfortunately, there's not much information available on him," she said. "It's tough to document. But when Dennis finally saw me, he said, "Oh. Yes, the high cheekbones!" I knew that I had Indian blood in me, and that Caesar had a Shawnee wife."

Caesar is so obscure that for years, people thought he was folklore. But Mr. Dalton determined that Caesar came to Southwestern Ohion with his owners in 1773 or 1774. When Indians killed them, Caesar escaped and lived in the wilderness.

"He was one of the earliest frontier explorers in this area," Mr. Dalton said. "The Shawnee took him in, and he lived with them at Old Town, their community near Xenia. The tribe adopted him and gave him a spot, and he built a house near a little tributary—now Caesar's Creek."

Mr. Dalton speculated that Caesar joined General George Rogers Clark's campaign against the British in Indiana about 1778 or 1779.

"Caesar showed Daniel Boone, one of my ancestors, escape routes," Mr. Dalton said.

Recently, he found records that suggest Caesar later moved to Lexington, Kentucky, and died at 80-90 years old. He was a strict Methodist in his last days, Mr. Dalton said, and probably was buried near Lexington.

A century and a half later, in the 1970s, the Army Corps of Engineers dammed Caesar's Creek and created the lake in Warren County. The corps obtained land for the park and leased it to the state. The Caesar Creek Pioneer Village Association subleased its land from the state, and added pioneer log buildings to create Pioneer Village.

Somehow, the federal government translated Caesar's Creek into Caesar Creek. That's not surprising, considering that some maps did the same.

Mr. Dalton has been irritated ever since.

"I've always wanted to see that misprint corrected." He said. "But I'm told there's no way. Bureaucrats probably think the place was named for Julius Caesar. Can you imagine the red tape involved in changing the name? We'd settle for a bronze marker.

"Pioneer Village has even offered to put one up. We hope to eventually have an interpretative library there."

Park spokeswoman Vinnie Ewing-Gibbings said she doesn't know how the grammatical error occurred.

"To get the name changed now would take a congressional order," she said.

Mrs. Donaldson, the family historian, isn't worried. She said she'd like to gather everything written about Caesar and place it at Pioneer Village.

Mr. Dalton said that is his goal, too, for Caesar represents a bridge between whites and blacks. "We've finally come together under the bonds of friendship," Mr. Dalton said.

Note: Caesar Creek lake is located in Warren, Clinton and Greene Counties in southwestern Ohio. The dam is on and 3 miles above the mouth of Caesar Creek, a tributary of the Little Miami River.

Tell Us What You Think
About the Black Dinosaurs™

Name _____

Address _____

City _____   State _____ Zip_____

Age _____   Grade _____

Who is your favorite Black Dinosaurs character?

_____

What topics would you like to see The Black Dinosaurs explore?

_____

_____

How did you get your first copy of Ziggy and The Black Dinosaurs™?
    (a) parent (b) gift © own purchase (d) other _____

Are you looking forward to the next title in The Black Dinosaurs™
series?
    (a) yes (b) no

If no, why? _____

_____

Comments?

_____

_____

_____

_____

Send your reply to: Author: The Black Dinosaurs™
                  c/o Just Us Books, Inc.
                  356 Glenwood Avenue
                  East Orange, NJ 07017